Tales from Mossy Bottom Farm

BLAST TO THE PAST

1977

1970

2008

1986

99

2006

First published 2016 by Walker Entertainment,
an imprint of Walker Books Ltd, 87 Vauxhall Walk, London SE11 5HJ

2 4 6 8 10 9 7 5 3 1

Written by Martin Howard and illustrated by Andy Janes
© and TM Aardman Animations Limited 2016. All rights reserved.
Shaun the Sheep (word mark) and the character Shaun the Sheep are
trademarks used under licence from Aardman Animations Limited.

This book has been typeset in Manticore

Printed and bound in Great Britain by Clays Ltd, St Ives plc

British Library Cataloguing in Publication Data:
a catalogue record for this book is available from the British Library

ISBN 978-1-4063-6623-5

www.walker.co.uk

Tales from Mossy Bottom Farm

BLAST TO THE PAST

Martin Howard

Illustrated by Andy Janes

WALKER
ENTERTAINMENT

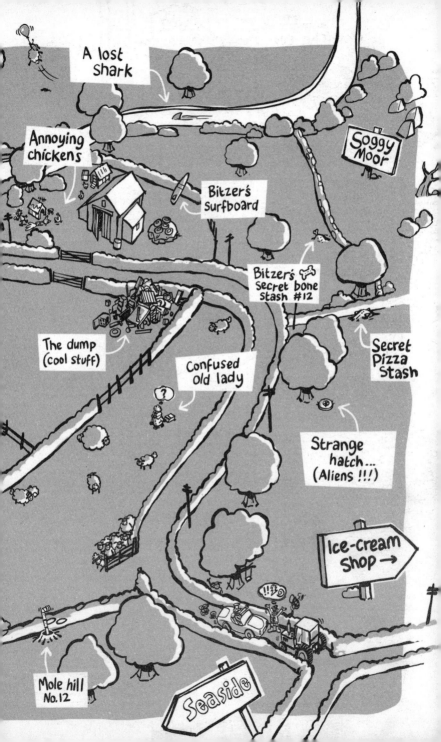

SHAUN is the leader of the Flock. He's clever, cool and always keeps his head when the other sheep are losing theirs.

BITZER

The Farmer's faithful dog and a good friend to Shaun, Bitzer's the ever suffering sheepdog doing his best to keep Shaun's pals out of trouble.

THE FARMER

Running the farm with Bitzer at his side, the Farmer is completely unaware of the human-like intelligence of his flock … and their shenanigans.

THE FLOCK

One big happy (if slightly dopey) family, the sheep like to play and create mischief together, though it's usually Shaun and Bitzer who sort out the resulting mess.

TIMMY

He may be the baby of the Flock, but Timmy is often at the centre of things. It's a good job his mum is always there to keep him safe.

TIMMY'S MUM

The very loving – if sometimes absent-minded – mother of Timmy, she is recognizable by the curlers in her fleece.

THE PIGS

Mocking, lazy and greedy, the pigs are always ruining Shaun's schemes and disrupting life on the farm.

CONTENTS

CHAPTER ONE:

THE MOSSY BOTTOM FLYER

Shaun the Sheep shoved a box aside, kicking up a cloud of dust in the loft of the barn. He was looking for little Timmy's favourite kite, and he knew it was here somewhere.

Aha! There it was, tucked into the corner. But, as Shaun reached for the kite, his hoof knocked against something hard. The kite was wedged against a picture frame, and inside was one of Shaun's favourite old photos.

Shaun smiled as he stared at the image. He wished he could go back to those carefree days, when the Farmer was happier and full of energy. Lately the Farmer was always too tired and grumpy for tickle fights. Shaun sighed and set the picture aside.

An hour later, as Timmy's kite looped and soared in the air, Shaun peered round the garden gate. A few feet away, the Farmer was bent over, grumbling to himself as he pulled weeds from a row of cabbages.

Snickering quietly, Shaun gazed at the Farmer's wide bottom. It was too good an opportunity to miss; it would be just like old times! He took a run up and playfully butted the Farmer's backside.

With a surprised waah, the Farmer fell, face-first, into the cabbages. He came up spitting dirt. Shaun threw himself forward, leaping at the Farmer's chest. *Play fight!*

"Rofferme," the Farmer grunted, pushing Shaun away. With a deep groan, the Farmer creaked to his feet, clutching his back. He whistled for Bitzer, but no sheepdog appeared. The Farmer shook his head, grumbling, and staggered away towards the kitchen.

CREAK!

Shaun watched him go with a disappointed bleat. Then he shook his head sadly and headed back to the meadow, where Timmy held on tight to his kite string, giggling. If the Farmer wouldn't play with Shaun, the least Shaun could do was play with Timmy. Together, they could come up with something really fun for the whole Flock to do.

As he wandered past Bitzer, who was nodding along to some groovy beats on his headphones, the wind dropped. Timmy's kite fell from the sky.

The little sheep bleated with shock as the kite plummeted into the junk heap. Tears welled up in his eyes.

Across the meadow, Shaun vaulted over the wall. It was okay: he would fetch it. A few moments later he was scrabbling up the mountain of rubbish, climbing over old mattresses, crates and a broken garden gnome. He could see the kite above him, its tail fluttering. He stretched out a hoof to grab it. Below, something moved beneath his hoof. The rubbish pile shifted. An old shoe bounced off his head.

That was just the start of the avalanche.

Bleating, Shaun was swept away on a wave of empty bottles and bald tyres and a basket of wax fruit. A mouse jumped on his head, then scrambled away as Shaun tumbled.

At the bottom of the heap, he blinked. Something bonked him on the head. Rubbing the bump, Shaun watched a rusty and wonky wheel from an old pram bounce to the ground and roll away. His bumped head forgotten, Shaun gazed at the wheel. A smile twitched at the corner of his mouth.

In his imagination, he added another wheel, then another two, then a driver's seat. The go-kart would be sleek and fast and shiny. It would have mirrors and fluffy dice and flames painted down the side. It would be the Best. Go-kart. Ever!

A breeze caught Timmy's kite. Rising from the rubbish heap, the kite dropped into Shaun's hooves. His grin widened. He had an even better idea! Racing after the wheel, he bleated in excitement.

A few days later, on the far side of the meadow, at the top of Roly Poly Hill, Shaun shielded his eyes against the sun. Far away in the distance, the tiny figure of the Farmer pottered out of sight behind the farmhouse. He was still bent over and clutching his back, Shaun noticed.

The coast was clear. Shaun turned and gave a thumbs up.

Shaded by an old oak tree, the Flock clustered round a go-kart, bleating oohs and aahs. At the centre of the crowd, Hazel twiddled a rusty spanner. With an excited bleat, she patted the kart and stood up. It was ready. Shaun grinned, looking down in awe at the Flock's creation.

Old pram wheels, a wooden box, handlebars from an ancient bike, an old car seat and various bits and bobs of old rubbish had been transformed. Nailed to a broomstick in the middle was Timmy's kite. Working round the clock, the sheep had engineered a dream of speed: the **MOSSY BOTTOM FLYER**.

The go-kart is perfect, Shaun told himself. The seat was ripped, three of the wheels were bent and there were no brakes except for a parachute that had been made from a stained sheet and some hairy string, but the most important thing was that it *looked* snazzy. Shirley had painted flames down the side – in green paint because no-one could find any red. The Twins had tied on a pair of rusty car wing-mirrors and an old, cracked shaving mirror. Timmy's Mum had knitted a pair of fluffy dice.

Shaun nodded to himself happily. There was no mistaking that the **MOSSY BOTTOM FLYER** was a speed machine.

Snapping on a pair of swimming goggles and tying on a colander crash-helmet, Shaun lowered himself into the driver's seat and tied a rope safety belt across his lap. Checking the mirrors, he pulled a lever. At the back of the kart a torch blinked on and off.

Hazel bleated. The indicator was working. All systems go. Shaun hunched over the handlebars, excitement glowing in his tummy. He peered through his goggles down Roly Poly Hill. The **MOSSY BOTTOM FLYER'S** route was lined with sheep waving flags made from sticks and the Farmer's underwear.

Tongue sticking out in concentration, Nuts gripped the back of the seat, ready to give the go-kart a shove off. Hazel bleated: Three ... two ... one ... GO! She waved a pair of chequered underpants.

A wheel fell off.

With an embarrassed bleat, Hazel fixed it back in place with a couple of thwacks of her spanner.

GO!

Nuts grunted with effort. Wind filled Timmy's kite, like a sail. The **MOSSY BOTTOM FLYER** began to move, picking up speed as it reached the brow of the hill. The kite's tail streamed out behind Shaun as he looked down on the farm spread out below him. Gritting his teeth, he tugged the handlebars, steering towards the distant figure of Bitzer. The sheepdog was plodding back from his favourite tree, staring at his newspaper and sucking a pencil.

Shaun sniggered. Bitzer would get a surprise when Shaun sailed past in the awesome machine.

24

25

In the meadow below, Bitzer stared at the crossword puzzle. Three down was a very difficult clue: "Four-legged, grass eating, woolly animal: five letters." He read the fiendishly hard clue again and cleaned out an ear with his pencil. What could it be?

Distant bleats interrupted his concentration. Annoyed, Bitzer looked up. A swaying tower of screaming sheep hurtled towards him at high speed.

Bitzer blinked. *Sheep!* Of course! That was the answer!

Turning back to the crossword, he started scribbling, then stopped. *A swaying tower of sheep,* he thought to himself. *That was unusual, wasn't it?*

Bitzer looked up again. The bleats were louder now, and the sheep were much, *much* closer. The out-of-control

MOSSY BOTTOM FLYER bounced over a molehill. Sheep clung desperately to each other as they flew into the air.

The newspaper and pencil dropped from Bitzer's paws. Clutching his hat with one paw and looking over his shoulder in fear, he ran.

Too late.

Far too late.

The **MOSSY BOTTOM FLYER** caught up with him, knocking him into the air. Bitzer's paws scrabbled at nothing for a moment and then clutched hold of Timmy's Mum. With a long whuuuuuuuuufffff, he glimpsed a stone wall. It came closer, and closer and...

KEEER-AAASSSH!

Everything went black.

CHAPTER TWO:

THE GOOD
OLD DAYS

A wheel rolled across the grass, making a sad, squeaky noise. Groans drifted across the meadow. Shaun sat up. Birds tweeted round his head. Annoyed, he waved a hoof until they flew off to a nearby tree, where they stared at him with beady eyes. From the back of the wrecked **MOSSY BOTTOM FLYER** came a small pffft sound. At last, the parachute popped out, covering Shaun in a smelly sheet.

By the time he untangled himself, the other sheep were getting to their feet, clutching their heads. Shirley pulled Timmy out of her fleece and gently put him on the grass with a pat on the head. Bitzer pulled his head from a rabbit hole with a faint pop. Timmy's Mum adjusted her curlers. Nuts hopped from one foot to another, bleating: Again, *again*!

From the corner of his eye, Shaun saw a figure walking round the corner of the farmhouse. Leaping to his feet, he gave an urgent bleat: *the Farmer!*

An instant later, the wreckage of the **MOSSY BOTTOM FLYER** had been stuffed into Shirley's fleece. Sheep stood around on four legs, munching grass as if nothing had happened.

The Farmer leaned over the wall, one hand scratching his head and the other holding a book.

Then grass fell from Shaun's mouth. He blinked. Had he hit his head too hard on the wall? Shaun tapped a hoof against his forehead in an attempt to get his brain working. He looked up at the Farmer once again.

The Farmer who was *not* the Farmer...

Shaun looked around. Bitzer and the rest of the Flock were all staring at the Farmer, too, jaws hanging open almost to their feet.

Earlier, at breakfast time, the Farmer had looked like his normal self: balding and slightly grumpy. Now, the thick glasses were the same, but he had a full head of red hair and a bushy beard. He was wearing a checked shirt with braces and – Shaun blinked again, not believing what he was seeing – he had an *earring*!

Giving the Flock a cheerful grin, the Farmer closed his book with a snap and strolled away whistling.

Shaun looked at Bitzer. Bitzer looked at Shaun. Shaun looked at Shirley. Shirley looked at Nuts. Nuts crossed his eyes and looked at both Twins. Slowly, they all shook their heads. Something had gone very, *very* wrong.

With a shocked bleat, Shaun pointed. On the gatepost where the cockerel usually stood was a small, yellow chick. It puffed out its chest, took a deep breath and tried to crow. The tiny cheep was drowned out by a clopping sound from the lane outside the farm. The animals' heads swung round to see an old-fashioned horse and cart trundle past. Along the side of the cart a sign read, "DAVEY MOSSIDGE: THE MOSSY BOTTOM GROCER".

Underneath, in smaller letters, were the words: "Get Mossidge's Sausages freshly delivered to your door: the *Modern* Way!" Shaun glimpsed two people sitting in the front. Both were wearing stripy blazers and straw hats. Then the horse trotted round the corner and the cart disappeared from view.

Sheep and sheepdog shared a look. A young farmer and baby cockerel? Horse-drawn carts? What did it all mean?

Shaun gulped. With a bleat, he pointed.

In the distance, the young Farmer was driving the tractor round in circles. Earlier that day it had been filthy and covered with mud, as usual. Now, its paintwork gleamed. It looked brand new. As the animals watched, the Farmer yanked the steering wheel, screaming. The tractor smashed through the front gate and off down the lane.

Shaun bleated again. An urgent meeting was called for.

Not long after, the Flock sat nervously in the grass while Shaun finished scribbling some very complicated maths on the chalkboard. None of the sheep noticed the curious eyes peeping over the wall that separated the meadow from the pigsty.

Shaun tapped the board. The sheep stared. Bitzer scratched his head as he tried to follow Shaun's equation.

The sheepdog hesitantly raised a paw.

Shaun peered at him and bleated: did Bitzer have a question?

Squirming, Bitzer whuffed and shrugged. Of course, he understood what the maths meant. But for the sake of the others, perhaps Shaun could explain it?

Rolling his eyes, Shaun rubbed out his workings and scribbled a diagram of the **MOSSY BOTTOM FLYER** racing down Roly Poly Hill. Next he drew a space-time vortex. Everyone could tell it was a space-time vortex because it was all wibbly-wobbly. Just to make sure, Shaun scrawled **"SPACE-TIME VORTEX"** at the top of the board and drew an arrow pointing to it.

Bitzer nodded. He had known there would be a space-time vortex involved all along.

Next, Shaun drew the **MOSSY BOTTOM FLYER** entering the space-time vortex and quickly sketched a young Farmer with all his hair and a pair of flared trousers. As he drew, he bleated quietly. It was really very simple: the **MOSSY BOTTOM FLYER** had been travelling at exactly the right speed to enter a space-time vortex, which had carried it – and all its passengers – back into the past.

The Flock had created a time machine! They had travelled back to the old days when people still used horses and carts and the Farmer was so young that he had only just started farming. The tractor was so new that he didn't even know how to drive it yet!

If any of the Flock had been listening carefully, they might have heard squealing whispers and giggles from the pigsty.

He he he HA he HE!

Nuts raised a hoof and bleated. If they had gone back in time, shouldn't there have been swirling tunnels of light and strange EYWOO-EYWOO noises?

No one had an answer to that.

Chapter Three:

COUNTRY LIFE

"Eywoo, eywoo."

Startled by the sound, the Flock pushed the chalkboard into a bush to hide Shaun's scribblings.

The gate creaked open and the hairy young Farmer clomped into the meadow wearing brand new wellington boots. "Eywoo," he repeated with an eager grin.

Shaun found himself grinning too, remembering head-butting the old Farmer into his cabbages. The young Farmer looked different. He wasn't grumpy, or moaning about his aching back. If the Flock had whizzed back through time into the past there might be some benefits, Shaun realized. Playfully, he butted the young Farmer's leg. Laughing, the Farmer bent down and wrestled Shaun onto his back, tickling him. Hazel pounced, and then Nuts and the Twins. Soon, the giggling Farmer was in the middle of a happy scrum of sheep. Shaun's head popped out with a bleat. It really *was* just like old times!

At an impatient bleat from Shirley, Bitzer stepped forward and dragged the Farmer from the hill of sheep by his hand. Holding out his clipboard, the sheepdog held it up in front of the red-faced, chuckling Farmer and tapped the front page. Whatever year it was, feeding time was feeding time.

Jumping to his feet, Shaun looked around the farm, wondering what other opportunities for fun the good old days might offer. His eyes lit up as he realized that he could make all the mischief he'd ever made all over again. And this time he'd know what to expect, especially from the cheating pigs. He glanced towards their sty, and blinked.

An enormous pig was leaning on the wall, wearing a lace bonnet and sucking a dummy. The pig winked at him. Shaun's mouth fell open. More proof that the Flock had time travelled! Even the pigs were tiny babies – no, *huge* babies, Shaun corrected himself.

His thoughts were interrupted by a frustrated whuff from Bitzer, who was waving his clipboard in the Farmer's face.

Ignoring the sheepdog, the Farmer pulled a book from his pocket. On the cover was a picture of a man who looked as though his beard had crawled up his face. He was proudly holding up a bunch of leaves. Underneath, in gold letters, were the words: **"COUNTRY LIFE: A GROOVY YOUNG PERSON'S GUIDE TO LIVING OFF THE LAND"**.

Licking a finger, the Farmer riffled through the pages. "A-ha," he said, jabbing with a finger. "Eeep." Looking down at Bitzer, he added, "Eepdob." After running a finger down the page, he cleared his throat, pursed his lips and let out an ear-splitting whistle.

Dropping his clipboard, Bitzer stared at him. Back on the Mossy Bottom Farm of the future, the Farmer whistled perfect sheepdog. Here, he had just whistled a command that meant "Fetch me a hat made by earwigs, this instant."

Seeing Bitzer's blank stare, the Farmer checked his book and whistled again. This time, he gave Bitzer the command to round the sheep up and serve them afternoon tea and sprouts in the greenhouse. He pointed to the door.

Bitzer blinked as understanding dawned. The Farmer was trying to tell him – very badly – to take the sheep to the feeding troughs. Nodding, he peeped his own whistle and began herding the sheep out.

A few minutes later, the Farmer emptied a sack of feed into a trough. Tossing the empty sack over his shoulder, he rubbed his hands together and said "Num-num-num-eh?" with a chuckle before clomping off.

The sheep stared at the mound of food. The Farmer had done everything right, but somewhere along the line he had picked up a sack of chicken feed rather than sheep feed. Shirley poked it with a hoof and took an experimental munch. A second later, she spat out seeds. With an *eeeww gross* face, she scraped her tongue.

In the yard, the Farmer had his nose wedged between the pages of COUNTRY LIFE again. After a few moments, he muttered, "Ilkytie." The Flock's eyes followed him, getting wider and wider as he fetched a bucket and marched into the bull's field.

The bull, too, was shocked. Very, *very* few people dared to wander across his field. Anyone who did usually ran away screaming and waving their arms as soon as they spotted him. As a rule, they did not stroll towards him whistling and jauntily swinging a bucket. He stood stock-still, watching the Farmer as if he had learned a new trick. It was the same look a cat might have given a juggling mouse on a bicycle.

The Farmer placed the bucket on the grass and reached underneath for the bull's udders. Grumbling to himself, he groped around.

The bull's tail twitched, dangerously.

Pulling his book from his pocket, the Farmer checked again. **COUNTRY LIFE** said cows needed milking, and the great beast in front of him seemed cow-like enough. But where were its udders? Tucking the book away, the Farmer rummaged around under the bull again.

The Flock and Bitzer winced as he grabbed and pulled at whatever he could find.

Shaun looked around. The rest of the sheep and Bitzer stared back at him. The young Farmer didn't know the difference between a cow and a bull. He was *rubbish* at farming!

Shaking his head, Shaun pointed the way back to the barn. When the door was safely closed he began scribbling on the board again. First, he drew a picture of the old Farmer with Mossy Bottom Farm behind him. Carefully, he added smiling faces: himself, Bitzer, Shirley, Timmy's Mum, Timmy and the rest of the sheep. The Farmer held up a big pile of money and looked happy – as he always did when he was holding a big pile of money.

Next, Shaun rubbed out the money and turned the Farmer's smile to a frown. Then – one by one – he rubbed out the animals he had drawn, and finally the farm itself. Looking around, he bleated grimly.

They must have come back to a point in time when the Farmer was just learning to farm. If he wasn't very good at it, he might decide to go off and do something else instead, like painting or playing trombone or being a professional balloon-model maker. And if that happened, there might be no Mossy Bottom Farm in the future for them to get back to. The old Farmer was often peculiar, but he knew how to farm. The young version would never make any money. Mossy Bottom Farm would be ruined, and if Mossy Bottom Farm was ruined history would change. They might never exist!

There was only one thing for it. They would have to work round the clock to mend the **MOSSY BOTTOM FLYER**. At the same time, they would have to help the Farmer until he learned how to run Mossy Bottom Farm.

SQUEEE!

Shaun peeked outside the barn. Leaning against a stone wall, a row of pigs stared back at him. All of them were wearing baggy nappies that looked like badly folded old towels. One waved a rattle at him while another cuddled a battered teddy to its massive pink cheek.

Shaun whistled under his breath. Baby pigs really were *massive*.

CHAPTER FOUR

WHEN FARMERS GO BAD

By the following morning the Farmer's beard had gone wild and was speckled with muck, his trousers were tattered, his wellingtons crusted with cowpats, and he was covered in bruises. He wasn't whistling any more. Shaun's attempts to play had been met with muttered grumbling and a firm hand pushing him away. Shaun and Bitzer glanced at each other as he ducked into the henhouse, egg basket in hand. It was a simple job. All he had to do was pick up eggs and carry them back to the farmhouse. Surely he couldn't mess that up.

When the Farmer emerged from the henhouse holding a basket of eggs and punching the air in victory, Bitzer and Shaun almost clapped. But then the Farmer tripped, the egg basket flew into the air and he fell flat on his face. Half a second later – crack, splot, crack, splot, crack, splot – the rain of falling eggs shattered all over him. Yolk dripping down his beard, the young man sat on the step of the henhouse, put his eggy face in his hands, and sobbed.

Shaun butted the Farmer's leg sympathetically with his head. Bitzer noticed Beryl the hen dozing on a roost nearby. Picking her up, he used her to wipe egg off the Farmer's face and then popped her gently back on her roost. Slowly, the Farmer's blubbing stopped. With a faint smile, he patted Bitzer on the head and gave Shaun a stroke.

Bitzer tapped his clipboard. It was nearly eleven o'clock, and the farm's routines were very strict.

Eleven o'clock was sitting-in-the-deckchair-with-a-mug-of-tea time. Pointing towards the kitchen, he whuffed firmly. It was a difficult job, but the Farmer had to do it.

While the Farmer sipped tea, his nose buried in **COUNTRY LIFE**, Shaun and Bitzer scattered food in the chicken run. By the time they returned to the farmhouse, the Farmer had fallen asleep in the deckchair, snoring. Shirley was standing beside him, scrawling in the Farmer's book.

Bitzer whuffed and held out a paw. Shirley, looking sheepish, handed the book over. Flicking through the pages, Bitzer noticed that in a section called **"CARING FOR**

SHEEP", she had crossed out some words and scribbled in new ones. The page now read:

"In the wild, sheep eat grass. However, they will be stronger and fitter if you give them ~~organic feed~~ Peetza, eyes-kream and kake.

Sighing and shaking his head, Bitzer crossed Shirley's changes out.

Curious, Shaun took the book from his paws and turned its pages, shuddering when he spotted a chapter on sheep shearing. **COUNTRY LIFE** wasn't just an instruction book, it was a complete guide to living off the land! Chuckling, he pointed to the section on finding wild food, which came with recipes for Stinging Nettle Omelette, Acorn

Cappuccino, Mushroom Porridge, Hogweed Salad and a load of other revolting dishes. *Bleugh.* Shaun made a face.

Bitzer grabbed the book back and riffled through the pages. He gulped. No wonder the Farmer was so useless. There was loads of stuff about farming, but nothing at all about the importance of nice, clean wellington boots. Instead, there were lots of silly chapters with headings like "**GROWING GREAT PRODUCE**" and "**HARVEST TIME**". The sheepdog snorted in disgust. How could anyone hope to become a good farmer without well-shined wellingtons?

Carefully, he placed the book in the Farmer's lap and pulled Shaun away. While the Farmer was sleeping, the pigs needed mucking out, and the ducks would get testy if their lunch didn't arrive on time. After that, they could weed the garden and mend the gate.

Together, Bitzer and Shaun marched off to work. A few moments later, Bitzer returned, a sly look on his face. Picking up the Farmer's book, he opened it to the section on looking after farm animals and found a section called "CARING FOR YOUR SHEEPDOG". Underneath the heading, he quickly started scribbling a new entry:

STEP ONE:
The importance of Bones!

CHAPTER FIVE:

HARD WORK!

Clang-a-lang-a-clang. The Farmer banged on an old tin bath with a stick. Breakfast time!

Shaun dragged himself out of bed. It felt like he had been asleep for only ten minutes, because he *had* been asleep for only ten minutes. He clutched his aching back and groaned while glancing at himself in the cracked mirror. His fleece was mucky, and he had bags under his eyes.

Then he peered over at the shape of the **MOSSY BOTTOM FLYER** hidden under a tarpaulin. After yet another all-night session with welding masks and flying sparks and nuts and bolts and screws, the go-kart was almost fixed and ready to take the animals back to the future. But they couldn't leave yet: every day brought a new farming emergency. And every day, the Farmer tried a new recipe from his **COUNTRY LIFE** book. The results had ranged from disastrous to catastrophic.

The last three days had gone like this...

DAY ONE

After reading in **COUNTRY LIFE** that scientists thought plants grow faster to music, the Farmer played guitar and wailed in the vegetable garden until the vegetables lost the will to live.

He wasn't the only one wailing: the pig babies cried and squealed until food was brought out to them. The Flock spent all day ferrying food from the kitchen to the pigsty just to get some peace and quiet.

Then the Flock spent the whole night feeding fresh manure and water to the poor, shrivelled veg, until the withered plants decided life might be worth living after all. While the Farmer slept, Shaun sneaked into his bedroom and snipped the strings of his guitar.

The farmer's dinner:

After carefully picking stinging nettles, the Farmer had tried making Stinging Nettle Omelette. But the recipe had gone wrong, leaving the Farmer screaming with nettle stings until his tongue had swollen up like a balloon. The Flock hoped this meant he couldn't sing the next day.

DAY TWO :

The Farmer read that animals' instincts are to forage for their own food as Nature intended, so he went round the farm leaving gates open. Shirley wandered off to Mossy Bottom Village where she foraged as Nature intended – by gobbling Sweet and Sour Noodles from customers' plates in **MR CHUNG'S CHINESE RESTAURANT**. The chickens foraged as Nature intended by descending in a flock on Old Mrs Badlegg's tea and seed-cake party. Nappy-wearing pigs waited until the Farmer went to market then foraged as Nature intended for the last of the frozen pizza in the farmhouse kitchen.

Bitzer and Shaun rounded up most of the animals, poking, prodding and (in Shirley's case) rolling them back to their homes. One of the baby pigs had been so full of pizza that Bitzer had tried to put it over his shoulder and pat its back. It let out a mighty burp that shook the farmhouse windows.

Soon after the Farmer returned from the market, he was visited by a stream of angry neighbours, including Mr Gasper from down the road, who was leading the Farmer's goat, Mowermouth, on a piece of string. A scrap of Mr Gasper's hallway carpet was still caught between Mowermouth's teeth.

The Farmer's dinner:

Snail Delight, which had escaped, very slowly, through an open window.

DAY THREE

The Farmer tried to plough the bottom field. Most farmers plough in straight lines up and down the field, but the Farmer ploughed a single furrow that stretched through the front garden, up the lane, across the bottom field, through the woods on the other side and around Soggy Moor three times before returning towards the farm and ploughing through a wall then heading towards the sheep dip. Luckily, the tractor ran out of petrol before the Farmer could try ploughing the sheep dip.

Once again, Shaun and Bitzer were up all night putting everything right while the Farmer snored. Next morning, they watched him scratch his head as he stared at the field. It now had neat, straight furrows, and a painted sign that had been planted in the mud.

The Farmer's dinner:

Wild Garlic Surprise, which had not one but *two* surprises. The first surprise was that it exploded in the pan, painting the kitchen ceiling in lumpy, grey goo. The second surprise was that after the Farmer scraped some off the ceiling and ate it, the Wild Garlic Surprise did some *very* surprising things to his tummy. The smell had followed him round Mossy Bottom Farm all evening.

DAY FOUR

Shaun groaned to himself as he surveyed the farm. His whole body was sore, and he felt homesick for the easy living of the future.

The Farmer passed Shaun on his way to the barn, and he tried to start a play fight. Grumbling under his breath, Shaun pushed the Farmer away. He was too tired for fun.

A grouchy-looking Bitzer peeped his whistle and turned his **"STOP"** sign to **"GO"**. Shaun trooped across the lane with the rest of the Flock. *It wasn't all bad news,* he told himself. After three days, the Farmer had finally noticed that the feed bags contained different types of food for different animals, thanks to large signs with pictures of sheep and chickens and arrows that pointed to the right bags.

The baby pigs still needed to be specially fed, however. They had become pickier, erupting in loud sirens of cries until fresh whipped cream was brought for their double-fudge ice-cream sundaes.

In the distance a familiar sound of clanking machinery started up. Chewing a mouthful of feed, Shaun groaned again. The Farmer had switched on the hay baling machine. Shaun squeezed his eyes closed, expecting the worst.

Sure enough, after only a few seconds the baling machine began making a juddering noise. There was a loud bang. Then a scream. The Farmer tottered out of the barn, his arms and legs poking out of a hay bale. Shaun couldn't help noticing that his beard had been neatly baled, too.

Yet another problem to sort out...

CHAPTER SIX:

SURPRISES AND HAIRCUTS

Slowly but surely, the Flock's hard work began to pay off. Yes, there were a few teeny problems – on day five the Farmer had blown up the shed, then fallen through the roof of the barn, and on day six he got his beard caught in the wheelbarrow – but after only a week the farm was running like clockwork. All the plants were alive, and the Farmer had just finished ploughing the top field in almost straight lines. While Shaun and Bitzer watched, he parked by the farmhouse door by pulling a lever on the tractor controls where the word **"BRAYKE"** had mysteriously appeared in chalk. Behind him was only one broken fence, which a team of exhausted sheep quickly mended. The Farmer gave the tractor a quick polish and wandered into the kitchen.

Shaun gave a tired but happy bleat. The future was safe. It was time for them all to go home. Someday soon, once the Farmer shaved his silly beard off, he would buy a flock of lambs and a puppy called Bitzer.

Shirley nudged him, rubbing her tummy. Could they hold off leaving until the Farmer had fed them? They might time-travel to the future and find themselves *hours* away from the next meal.

The rest of the sheep bleated in agreement. They didn't want to miss breakfast.

Bitzer stood by the kitchen door next to a pair of freshly cleaned wellington boots, and saluted. The door flew open. The sheepdog was flattened against the wall. Looking green in the face, the Farmer rubbed his gurgling tummy and heaved a bag of sheep feed over his shoulder.

Hungrily, the Flock trooped across the lane for breakfast.

A few minutes later, Shaun heard a horribly familiar sound. A horribly familiar sound that hadn't been caused by the Wild Garlic Surprise. He looked up from the trough. Food fell from his mouth. With a gulp, he backed away from the nightmare in front of him.

...BZZZZZZZ...

The Farmer had found the shearing clippers. Waving them in one hand, he strolled across the meadow with a grin on his face and **COUNTRY LIFE** open in his spare hand.

He was going to try shearing!

There was only one thing Shaun could do. With a bleat of terror, he jumped behind the massive bulk of Shirley.

So did the rest of the Flock.

...BZZZZ...BZZZZ...BZZZZ

As strong hands reached out and grabbed him, Shaun's bleating laughter was cut off with a gurgle.

"Oorgo," chuckled the Farmer.

Shaun struggled, the hideous buzzing of the clippers filling his ears.

He clenched his teeth, waiting...

In the distance, Shaun heard the clip-clop of a horse's hooves. "Oioioi!" shouted the Farmer. Hardly daring to hope, Shaun opened one eye. A second later, with a tiny pop, the other opened.

Jolting along the lane was the **DAVEY MOSSIDGE** grocery cart. The Farmer waved. Dropping the clippers, he jogged away, shearing forgotten.

Shaun bleated urgently: the Flock couldn't stay in the past a second longer. They had to get to the **MOSSY BOTTOM FLYER**!

The Flock didn't need telling. Shaun was almost trampled in the stampede for the gate.

Seconds later, Shaun peered round the barn door. The Farmer had disappeared round the other side of the house. Shaun heard voices. A frown crossed his face: one of them sounded familiar. For a moment he thought he had already returned to the future. But it couldn't be... Shaun shook his head. The important thing was that the coast was clear.

With a squeaking of rusty wheels, the **MOSSY BOTTOM FLYER** was pushed out into the yard. Shaun's heart leapt at the sight. The go-kart was almost as good as new. Except for the patches and rusty nails holding it together, the string tying the broomstick together, a large rip in Timmy's kite, the bent-out-of-shape handlebars and the springs poking through the driver's seat, he could hardly tell that it had been in a crash.

A wheel fell off. Hazel fixed it back in place with a couple of thwacks from her spanner.

As the sheep and Bitzer pushed the vehicle towards the meadow, Shaun heard a squeee behind him. He turned to see a row of baby pigs leaning against the wall, all wearing little bonnets and grinning grins that looked much too wicked to belong to piglets. One of them blew a raspberry at him.

Shaun stopped. He frowned. Now he came to think about it, the baby pigs really were *enormous*. And they didn't really act like babies. There was something not quite right...

Bitzer grabbed him by the shoulder and pushed him towards Roly Poly Hill.

The **MOSSY BOTTOM FLYER** was ready for its journey through time. The Flock was going home.

CHAPTER SEVEN:

BACK TO THE FUTURE

At the top of Roly Poly Hill, Shaun shielded his eyes against the sunshine with a hoof and peered at the farmhouse. The horse and cart were still parked on the far side. The Farmer was out of sight and the coast was clear. He lifted his hoof and gave a thumbs up. Pulling on his goggles, he tied the colander helmet beneath his chin and turned to face the **MOSSY BOTTOM FLYER**.

The go-kart was packed with sheep. The Flock had formed a pyramid that sprouted arms and legs and faces – a pyramid that swayed dangerously in the breeze.

Shaun scrambled to the top. Timmy's Mum protested as his hoof squashed her curlers. Making himself comfortable on the Twins, Shaun looked around and bleated. From up here he could see all the way to the Big City.

Reaching for the handlebars, he bleated again. Uh-oh, his arms were too short! He couldn't steer!

Below him another pair of hooves stretched out. Nuts grinned up. Everything was all right. He – Nuts – was in control.

Shaun's bleat of protest was cut off as the **MOSSY BOTTOM FLYER** began to move.

mole hill
for sale →

Shaun sat up. Tweeting happily, birds circled round his head. Annoyed, he flapped them away and bleated: didn't they have anything better to do?

The birds flew to the nearest tree, fluffed out their feathers and glared at him.

The rest of the Flock staggered to their feet, groaning, as a grin broke out on Shaun's face. At last! The space-time vortex had brought them home, and dear old Mossy Bottom Farm was exactly as they'd left it!

Bitzer frowned, and whuffed. He pointed. Mossy Bottom Farm *was* exactly the same as they'd left it in the past. The tractor was shiny and polished, the vegetable patch freshly weeded and the fields ploughed in slightly wriggly lines. With a clopping of hooves, a horse pulled the old-fashioned grocery cart advertising **MOSSIDGE'S SAUSAGES** down the lane. A small chick climbed on the gatepost, puffed its chest out and cheeped.

Shaun's mouth fell open. They were stuck in the past!

Then he remembered the voice he had heard from behind the farmhouse, and the pigs...

The pigs.

Shaun glanced towards the pigsty where the pigs were leaning against each other laughing and pointing at the Flock. One spat out its dummy, clutching its sides laughing. The lace bonnet slipped from the head of another.

He blinked. Without their bonnets and dummies, the pigs didn't look much like babies at all. In fact, they looked just like pigs who had been wearing disguises.

But that would mean... Shaun's mouth
dropped open. *No*, he told himself. *It wasn't
possible. He had done the maths and everything.*

Bitzer whuffed again. This time his paw
pointed to an unexpected sight. Round the
corner of the farmhouse walked *two* farmers:
one young with a beard and long hair and
an earring, the other older, balder and clean-
shaven. The second Farmer was wearing an
old-fashioned stripy blazer and a straw hat. In
his hand was a suitcase that had been covered

in stickers. The biggest read, "**THE LOWER PIDDLINGTON HISTORY FAIR!**" Under one arm, the Farmer was carrying a small tin cup onto which had been engraved the words "**EIGHTH PRIZE IN THE OLDEN DAYS FANCY DRESS COMPETITION**". For once, he wasn't clutching his aching back. He looked happy and well rested. Leaning over the gate, he grinned and stretched over to tickle Shaun.

Shaun could only stare back. He tried to bleat but nothing came out. If both Farmers were there then that meant...

At the sound of a small scuffle, his head swung round. On the gatepost, the cockerel pushed his grandson aside, coughed, filled his chest and began to crow. At the end, he gave the chick a wink. *That* was how you did it!

Shaun looked back to see the entire Flock and Bitzer glaring at him. Timmy's Mum crossed her arms. She bleated: it had taken her three whole nights to weed the vegetables. Her hooves were killing her. Hazel tutted. She'd almost put her back out baling hay.

A grumble went around the Flock, getting louder as each sheep added new complaints.

Nuts bleated. He didn't know what everyone was moaning about. He'd really enjoyed travelling back in time. Everything had been better back then. Even the air smelled fresher in the past.

Angry bleats filled the air. They hadn't *been* to the past! The Farmer had just gone on holiday to a history fair for a week. He and his friend from the village had dressed up in old-fashioned clothes and driven there on an old horse-drawn cart. The tractor wasn't new, the young Farmer had just polished it.

Shaun and his silly equations had got everything wrong!

Bitzer growled. He had wondered why the young Farmer hadn't been surprised when a flock of sheep and a sheepdog had appeared out of nowhere. Hazel made an annoyed face. *She* had wondered why the bull and Mowermouth the goat had come back to the olden days when they hadn't been on the **MOSSY BOTTOM FLYER**.

Shaun tried a sheepish grin. Bitzer and the Flock still glared at him. He shuffled his feet, and bleated. It wasn't his fault. Everyone knew how easy it was to fall into a space-time vortex...

In the yard, the old Farmer had put his arm round the young Farmer's shoulder as he looked around the neat and tidy farm. With a chuckle, he slapped the younger version of himself on the back. Reaching into his jacket, he pulled out his wallet and counted out some money, then changed his mind and shoved most of it back. The remaining notes, he held out to his nephew.

The nephew's tummy gurgled. He hadn't eaten anything for a week other than Wild Garlic Surprise, foraged acorns, and leaves and wild mushrooms still covered in cowpat. He took **COUNTRY LIFE** from his pocket, tossed it over his shoulder and tapped a number into his mobile phone.

Mowermouth the goat sniffed at the book, then ate it in two bites.

Leaving the Farmer's nephew gabbling into the phone at top speed, Bitzer and the Flock turned their backs on Shaun and stalked off with their noses in the air. On the other side of the wall, the pigs were still laughing hysterically. Bitzer whuffed crossly under his breath. Shaun and his stupid space-time vortex had cost everyone a week's sleep!

With a sigh, Shaun stared through the bars of the gate, just as the Farmer shot out of the kitchen door. The Farmer's happy smile had vanished. Now, his face was as red as a tomato. He looked as if he was about to explode. *Maybe he had tried some Wild Garlic Surprise,* Shaun thought to himself, glumly.

"Oiwarraoodunmekishen?" the Farmer roared.

Shaun's mouth made an ooooo shape. He had forgotten about the mess in the kitchen. Snail Delight had crawled into the drawers. Wild Garlic Surprise hung like smelly stalactites from the ceiling. The floor was ankle deep in Acorn Cappuccino. The walls were covered in soot, and one end of the kitchen table had gone up in flames. The food processor would never process again, and there was a hard-boiled egg wedged into the toaster. The oven would probably have to be scrapped.

The Farmer's nephew swung round with a jump and saw his uncle striding towards him with a face like thunder. Making a terrified gurgling sound, he dropped the pile of cash and ran for the bus stop where – luckily – a bus was just about to close its doors. He was still waving from the back window as the bus pulled away with the Farmer in hot pursuit.

Chapter Eight:

AN UNEXPECTED REWARD

Shaun stood by the front gate, watching as the bus got smaller and smaller with the tiny speck of the Farmer chasing it. He sighed again. He had been so sure that the Flock had travelled in time, and the maths had proved it. *Maybe,* he thought to himself, *he had multiplied x by a pound sign when he should have divided y by a love heart.*

Looking over his shoulder, he watched the Flock trudging back to the barn with the remains of the **MOSSY BOTTOM FLYER**. The Twins yawned. Bitzer dragged his feet, dog-tired. Shaun's stomach rumbled. *They hadn't even had time to finish breakfast,* he told himself, miserably. And it was all his fault.

Toot toot.

Shaun blinked at a familiar sight – a spotty boy with glasses on a red moped. On the back was a large red box. After checking the address, the pizza boy tooted his horn again. Shaun's stomach rumbled again.

Grumpily, the pizza boy leaned on the horn of his moped. A long tooooooot rolled across the meadow. Still no one came to pick up the delivery. Muttering to himself, he revved the engine and turned to make sure there were no cars coming before he pulled away. Strangely, the box on the back of his moped was open. The pizzas he had come to deliver had been replaced with a pile of money. Shaking his head over the mystery, the pizza boy drove away.

Behind the hedge, Shaun sniffed at the pizzas the young Farmer had ordered on his mobile phone. Clearly, a week of foraged food had left the young man hankering for thick, delicious melted cheese.

Shaun looked up again. Far away, the bus disappeared over the top of a hill. *The young Farmer wouldn't be coming back any time soon,* he told himself. Plus, the Flock and Bitzer *had* spent a week doing most of the work around the farm. Tomorrow they would roughhouse with the well-rested and re-energized Farmer. But tonight, they deserved a reward...

The barn door opened with a creak. Shaun peered round it. Bitzer and the Flock gave him cold stares.

Shaun grinned and dropped a pile of pizzas on a bale of hay. The smell of melted cheese filled the barn.

Shirley bleated. She'd *always* thought Shaun was a *brilliant* sheep. The best. Totally awesome. A sheep in a million.

Bleats of agreement shook the barn. They died away quickly and were replaced by the noises of sheep and sheepdog chewing, and sucking dribbles of tomato sauce off their paws and hooves.

Shaun sat on an upturned bucket. His cheeks bulging, he pointed a half-eaten slice of Quadruple Cheese with Extra Cheese at the wreckage of the **MOSSY BOTTOM FLYER**.

Through a mouthful of pizza, he bleated: with a few tweaks, the Flock might just be able to get it working. They could become *real* time travellers.

Bitzer frowned, waving his own slice in a gesture that asked, "Why?"

Munching away, Shaun thought about it for a moment.

He swallowed, then bleated happily. Bitzer was right. In all of time and space there was nothing better than being right here, right now.

ACTIVITIES

MAKE YOUR OWN TIME CAPSULE

A space-time vortex is very hard to find – it usually involves hypermolecular lenses and hairy string – but you can bridge the past and the future in a much simpler way: a time capsule! Below are instructions for sending memories to your future self.

◆ SET YOUR FUTURE TARGET

Pick a date in the future for when the time capsule should be unsealed. Is it one year from now, five years – or even ten years from now? The longer the wait, the greater the risk that the container won't survive into the future, or that it will be forgotten. On the other hand, the longer the wait, the more rewarding it will be to open! If you can't decide, make several different capsules, each for a different target date.

◆ FIND A SUITABLE CONTAINER

You need to work out how you will store the capsule safely. If you plan to bury it underground, make sure the container is watertight, ideally made of stainless steel or another sturdy material that can withstand moisture. You may store the capsule indoors, perhaps in an attic, or in the back of a wardrobe. In any case, make sure to clearly label the capsule with its target date to avoid any early unsealing by someone tidying up or digging in the garden!

◆ COLLECT EVERYDAY ITEMS

Now it's time to start putting together the contents of the capsule. Photos, medals and stuffed animals are a few suggestions. Avoid anything digital that needs to be opened on a device – the formats will likely be very different in the future!

◆ WRITE A LETTER

Write to the future you, telling yourself all about life today. Describe your friends, your worries, your hopes and your daily life. Everyday details are best, since they are probably the things you are most likely to forget. Ask questions! Give yourself some advice!

◆ SEAL THE CONTAINER AND STORE IT

The hardest part comes after the time capsule is safely stored away: remembering to open it! Can you think of ways to remind yourself about the time capsule, far off in the future? (Other than going through a space-time vortex, that is.)

HOW TO DRAW THE FARMER

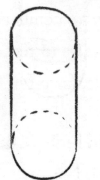

STEP 1 Draw two circles, one on top of the other. Connect the sides, forming a pill shape.

STEP 2 Add three smaller circles in a line near the top. These will be his nose and ears.

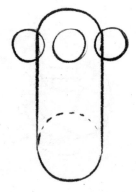

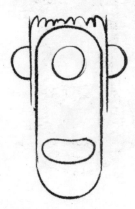

STEP 3 Make hair by drawing lines on either side of the top half of the pill, topped by a bumpy line. Add a bean-shaped mouth.

STEP 4 Draw rectangles at the tops of the ears for the Farmer's glasses. Divide the mouth with a line.

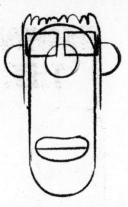

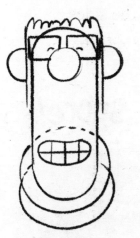

STEP 5 Add little arches for eyes, and three vertical lines for teeth. Start the collar with two rings around his chin.

STEP 6 Add curves to define his ears. Round off his teeth and add texture to his hair and clothes. Hey presto!

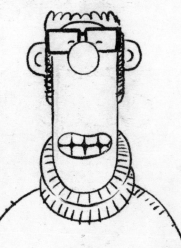